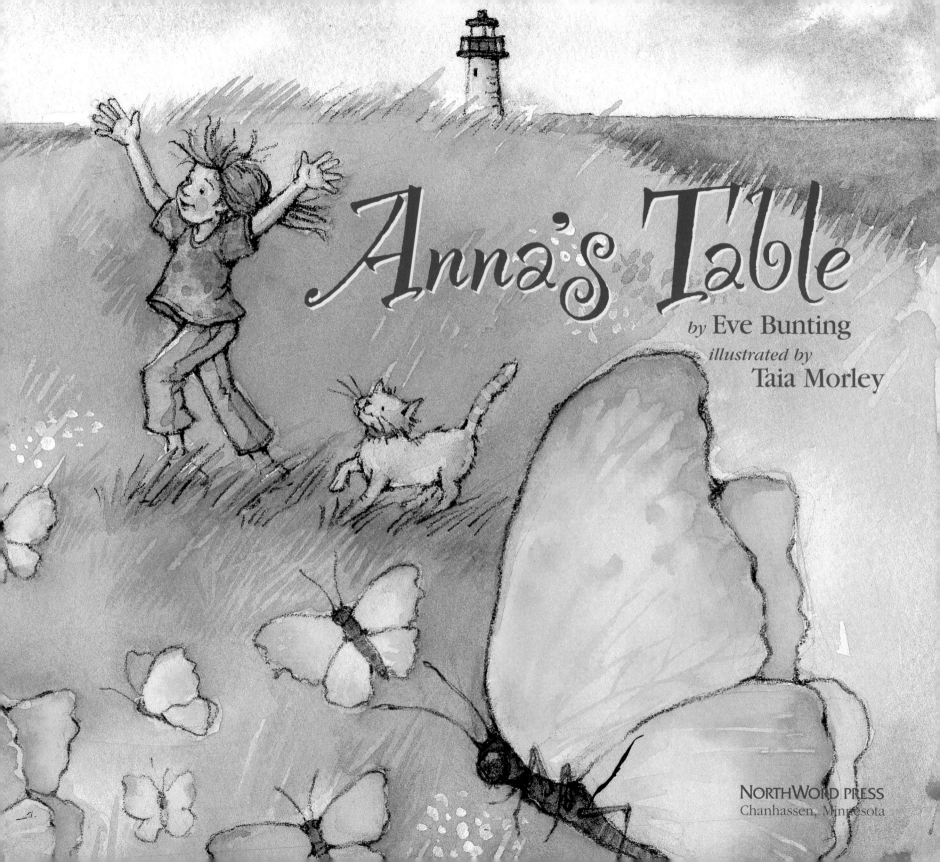

Anna's Table

by Eve Bunting

illustrated by
Taia Morley

NORTHWORD PRESS
Chanhassen, Minnesota

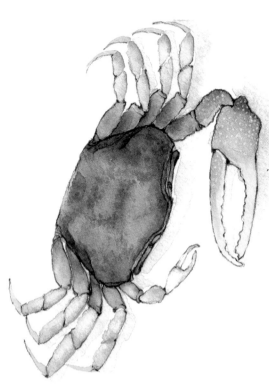

The text and display type were set in Garamond, Berkeley, and Remedy Double
Composed in the United States of America
Designed by Lois A. Rainwater
Edited by Aimee Jackson

Books for Young Readers
NorthWord Press
18705 Lake Drive East
Chanhassen, MN 55317
www.northwordpress.com

Library of Congress Cataloging-in-Publication Data

Bunting, Eve, date.
Anna's table / by Eve Bunting ; illustrations by Taia Morley.
p. cm.
Summary; Anna describes the collection of natural things she keeps on the table in her bedroom.
ISBN 1-55971-841-2 (hc.)
[1. Nature—Fiction. 2. Collectors and collecting—Fiction.] I. Morely, Taia, ill. II. Title.

PZ7.B91524 An 2002
[E]—dc21
2002032616

Printed in Singapore
10 9 8 7 6 5 4 3 2 1

To my granddaughter, Anna
—E.B.

For Tony
—T.M.

My Aunt Em knows
how much I love all nature things.
And so she bought a table
for my room.

On it I have a jar of beach rocks,
smooth and cool,
the color of the sea
when there are clouds.

I have a Fiddler crab,
long dead,
its back like crumpled tissue
and its coral legs hinged.
Touch them with care
or they might tear.

I have a spiral shell
that held a mollusk once.
My dad went in the ocean,
shoes and all,
to bring me this.

And then,
a big wave came
bigger than Dad.
He disappeared.
We cheered
when he appeared again
holding the shell
above his head.
"Our hero!" Mother said.

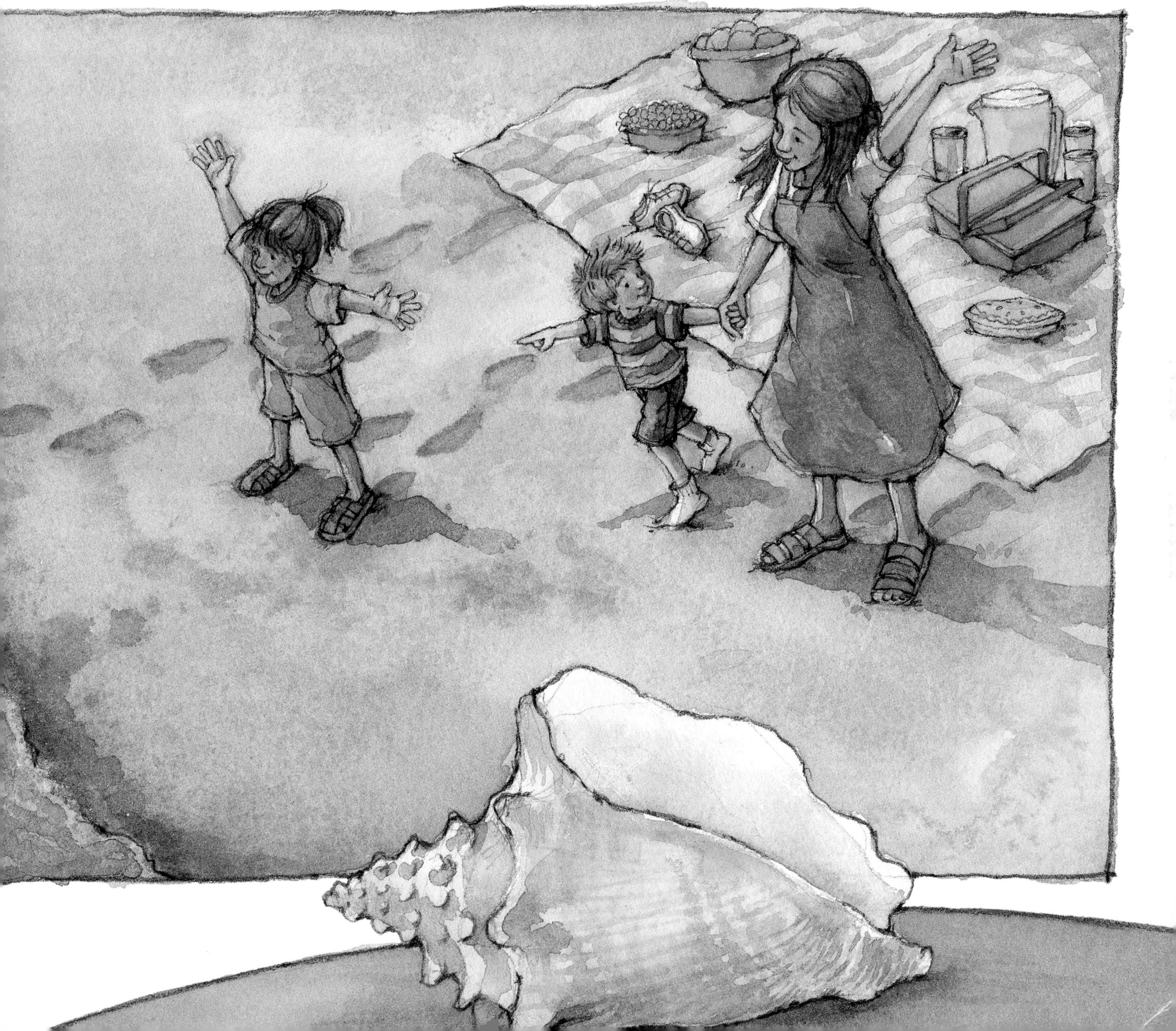

In my room against the wall
I have a nature table.
On it I have a seahorse,
elegant and small.
He could be wax,
not real at all.

I have a box of tiny bones
that came, I think,
from some poor mouse.
They were in owl pellets
that I found
scattered around
the oak tree by my house.
Poor little mouse.
But Dad says this is nature's way.
An owl must eat to stay alive.
Must hunt just to survive.

I have a caterpillar,
curled and mummy black.
A lizard,
thin and wide,
run over by a car.
"Just see how carefully
it's made.
See how my lizard is as pale a shade
as jade,
and just as beautiful!"

I have a seagull's skull
I found once
buried in the sand.

I have a piece of bark
shaped like a hand,
its fingers
long and thin
as those of Miss Lenore.
She teaches me guitar
and says
I would be good
if I would practice more.

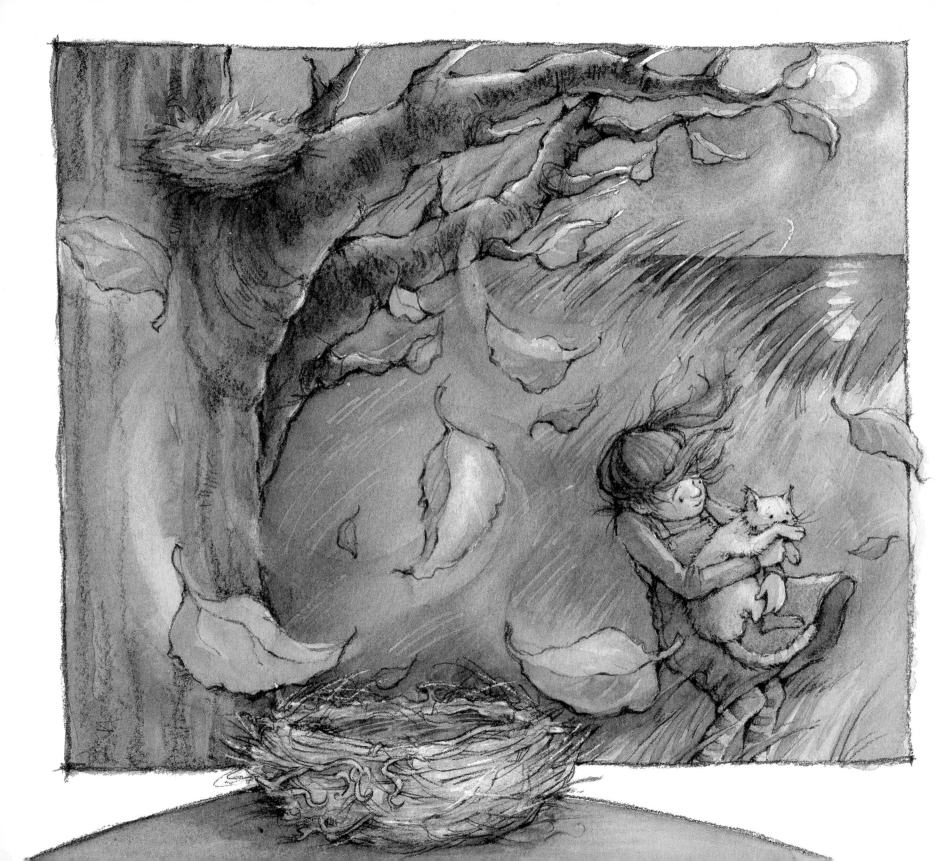

I have two dried and dusty nests
that fell
one windy night.

I have a shark's tooth
and a geode,
cracked across
so I can see
the crystal crumbs inside.

I have a blue jay's feather
and the backbone
of a garter snake
that looks like puckered ribbon,
and a dried up honeybee,
no longer striped,
so white
that it could be a daisy head
instead.
I hold it.
And I think
how once it flew
among the flowers
and buzzed away the hours.

I have a pomegranate,
hard and dry.
I saved this one.
My mom and dad
made jelly from the rest.
"That jelly's
much too beautiful
to spread
on bread," Dad said.
"What we have here
are jars of liquid light."
"You're right," Mom said.
We ate it, every bite.

I have a drift of butterflies,
their colors orange bright.

We found them in the grass
one night
after a cold strong wind
and sudden freeze
swept them from the trees.
The butterflies arrive
each spring
in Lighthouse Park,
and rest
before they rise again
and fly to southern skies.
These will fly no more
forever.

My mom came home
and got my basket, padded it with ferns
so they would have
a nature bed.
"We'll put them on your table,"
Mother said.

Sometimes I take a treasure
to my school
to show my friends
how clever nature is.
How bone fits into bone,
each to its own.

The beauty of a river stone.

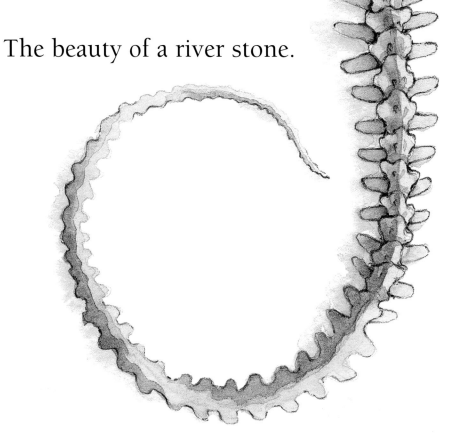

In my room
against the wall
I have a nature table
filled with the wonders
of the earth
and sky and sea.

Each one of them
a miracle to me.

EVE BUNTING is the author of over 200 books for children, including the 1995 Caldecott-winning *Smoky Night*, illustrated by David Diaz. Her many honors include the Golden Kite Award from the Society of Children's Book Writers; the Southern California Council on Literature for Children and Young People Award; the PEN Literary Award for Special Achievement in Children's Literature; the American Library Association's Best Books for Young Adults award; the Southern California Council on Literature for Children and Young People Excellence in a Series Award; the Edgar, given by the Mystery Writers of America; Writer of an Outstanding Social Science Book for Children award, given by the National Science Teachers Association and the Children's Book Council; and recognition by the Commonwealth Club of California.

Ms. Bunting was born in Northern Ireland and moved to the United States with her husband, Ed, at the age of 30. She began writing books for children at age 40 and continues to write every spare minute.

Ms. Bunting and her husband live in southern California. They have four grandchildren, one of whom is Anna.

TAIA MORLEY graduated from Cornell University with a degree in environmental and product design, and has had an array of fascinating jobs since then. She was a window dresser for Macy's NYC, and currently has a job most kids dream about: toy designer! She has designed toys for many different companies including Mattel, Hasbro, and Fisher-Price. Today she and her husband have a design business where she continues to design toys and packaging for toys.

Ms. Morley lives in Minnesota with her husband, their four children, one brown dog, lots of mosquitoes, toads, and countless other woodsy creatures. *Anna's Table* is her first picture book.